PRACTICE MAKES PERFECT
Robert Can Learn To Do Anything

D. J. Eva

Copyright © 2014

All rights reserved. No part of this book may be reproduced or transmitted in any form or by any electronic or mechanical means, including photocopy, recording, or any information storage and retrieval system now known or to be invented, without written permission from the publisher or author

Once there was a little boy. His name was Robert and he was seven years old.
One day he was playing with his friend, Mark.

"Look what I can do," said his friend Mark. "I can juggle."
Mark was able to juggle three oranges at one time.
"Wow. I wish I could do that," said Robert.

Robert tried and tried, but no matter how hard he tried, he couldn't do it. Every time he threw two or three oranges up into the air, he dropped them.

He got upset so he went home.

When he got home, he told his mom, "Mom, my friend Mark can do this cool juggling trick with three oranges, but I can't do it!" he complained.

"Of course you can do it!" his mother exclaimed. "You can do anything with practice!"

So Robert went to his room and tried. He dropped the oranges but he tried again.

He continued to try but he kept dropping the oranges: one, two, three, the oranges fell to the floor and rolled under his bed. No matter how hard he tried, he couldn't do it.

He went back to his mom. "I still can't do it!" he complained.

"Practice makes perfect!" his mother told him.

"Practice, keep trying, and soon you will be able to do it!"

So Robert went back up to his room and tried once again.
He threw one orange up into the air and caught it.
That was easy!

Then he threw the second orange up into the air and was able to catch both of them.
That wasn't too hard.

But every time he threw all three oranges up into the air one at a time, he ended up dropping not one, not two, but all three oranges!

He went to his mom. "I keep practicing, but I still can't do it!" he complained. "Practice makes perfect," she encouraged. "Keep practicing!"
"But it's so hard! When I try to do it, I can't do it!"
"When you try something new, you might fail at first," said his mom. "With practice you will be able to do it."

So, once again, Robert went to his room and tried. He threw one orange up into the air and caught it.

He threw two oranges up into the air and was able to catch both of them.

But every time he threw all the three oranges up into the air one at a time, he ended up dropping not one, not two, but all three oranges!

As he continued to practice, he thought that he was getting close to doing it, but he still couldn't do what his friend did.

He was good at catching two oranges, but catching the third orange was still very difficult.

He started to lose his patience! He went to his mom. "I still can't do it!"

"Don't give up, keep trying," said his mom. "Practice makes perfect."

So Robert went to his room. Each time he tried, he was getting close to doing it, but he still couldn't do what his friend did. He was good at catching two oranges, but catching the third orange was still very difficult.

He went to his mom. "I keep trying but I still can't do it!" he complained. "Practice makes perfect!" is all she said.

So Robert went back to his room.
He tried and he almost did it.
He tried and he almost did it.
He tried and he almost did it.

Finally, after trying many times, he was able to catch all three oranges, and throw them back up into the air, one at a time. He was juggling!

He was so excited. He quickly went to show his mom.

"Look: I can do it!" he said proudly.

"I told you," said his mom. "Practice makes perfect."

The next day, Robert went to school and showed all his friends.
He threw one orange up into the air, then the second, and finally the third.
He was juggling three oranges all at the same time!
All his friends were so amazed.
They cheered and clapped.

Some of his friends tried to do it, but they couldn't do it.
He was the only one who could do it at his school.

One of his friends asked, "How come you can do it and I can't?"
"Practice makes perfect," is all Robert said.
Robert realized there's nothing he couldn't do!

He learned to play the piano.

He learned to sing.

He learned to paint.

He learned to ice skate.

When anyone asked him why he was so good at doing things, "Practice makes perfect," is all Robert said.

Made in the USA
Middletown, DE
05 March 2018